A Day with

WILBUR
ROBINSON

WILLIAM JOYCE

Scholastic Inc.

New York   Toronto   London   Auckland   Sydney

LIBRARY OF CONGRESS CATALOGING-IN-PUBLICATION DATA

No part of this publication may be reproduced in whole or in part,
or stored in a retrieval system, or transmitted in any form or
by any means, electronic, mechanical, photocopying, recording,
or otherwise, without written permission of the publisher.
For information regarding permission, write to HarperCollins, Inc.,
10 East 53rd Street, New York, NY 10022.

ISBN 0-590-45579-6
ISBN 0-590-29097-5 (meets NASTA specifications)
Copyright © 1990 by William Joyce.
All rights reserved. Published by Scholastic Inc.,
730 Broadway, New York, NY 10003,
by arrangement with HarperCollins, Inc.

4 5 6 7 8 9 10   09   00 99 98 97

Printed in the U.S.A.   08

First Scholastic printing, April 1992

DEDICATION

For John Henderson Cade—a matchless pal
and Robinson to the core.
—W. J.

I was going to spend a day at Wilbur Robinson's house. Wilbur is my best friend. His house is the *greatest* place to visit.

I walked up and said hello to the twin uncles, Dmitri and Spike. As always, Wilbur opened the door just before I knocked.

"Come on in," he said. "Lefty will take your bag."

"It's kind of dull around here today," said Wilbur.

I looked around. Aunt Billie was playing with her train set, Cousin Pete was walking the cats, and Uncle Gaston sat comfortably in the family cannon.

"Your dad needs you out in the backyard," he shouted as he blasted himself across the room.

In the backyard, we found Mr. and Mrs. Robinson and their robot, Carl. They were scouring the lawn with the matter detector.

"We're looking for Grandfather's false teeth," Mr. Robinson explained. "Of course, we haven't seen *Grandfather* lately either," he added. "Could you boys go inside and ask around?"

Back inside, we found Uncle Judlow, relaxing with his brain augmentor.

"It helps him think deep thoughts," Wilbur whispered.

"Mississippi spelled with *o*'s instead of *i*'s would be *Mossossoppo!*" blurted Uncle Judlow.

"See? What did I tell you?" Wilbur exclaimed.

"Have you seen Grandfather Robinson's false teeth?" I asked.

Uncle Judlow blinked. "They're wherever he left them," he answered after some thought.

In the den, Wilbur's sister Tallulah was talking on the phone and eating grapes. His other sister, Blanche, was modeling her new prom dress.

"Do the shoes match?" she asked.

"They're swell," we chimed.

"Have you seen Grandfather Robinson's false teeth?" I asked.

"Or Grandfather?" asked Wilbur.

"Not lately," said Blanche.

Yawning, Tallulah shook her head and ate another grape.

"We're striking out," said Wilbur, discouraged. "And I'm hungry, so let's eat."

Cousin Laszlo came by to demonstrate his new antigravity device.

"Have you seen Grandfather Robinson's false teeth?" I asked.

"Nope, but I bet they're floating around here someplace," mused Cousin Laszlo.

Suddenly the faint familiar strains of "Potato Head Blues" came wafting from the house.

"That's it!" yelled Wilbur. "It's Friday—Grandfather's in his lab working with his dancing frog band!"

We rushed to the lab. Sure enough, there was Grandfather with his friends Mr. Ellington and Mr. Armstrong. Grandmother Robinson was helping.

"Have you found your teeth, Grandfather?" shouted Wilbur over the music.

"Nah, haven't theen 'em." He smiled.

"I guess we'll just keep looking," I volunteered.

"Thure do apprethiate it," said Grandfather as the music played on.

"We found Grandfather!" Wilbur announced as we ran outside.

"Good work!" said Mr. Robinson. "Now if we could only find those teeth!"

"Last time I was here, we were looking for your grandfather's glass eye," I reminded Wilbur as we walked.

"Yeah, he's always missing a part," Wilbur admitted.

"Ahoy!" called Uncle Art, newly arrived from abroad. "Looking for a lost bit of Grandfather? Gadzooks, I've been homesick."

By evening, Grandfather's teeth were still nowhere to be found.

At dinner, Uncle Gaston practiced shooting food out of a cannon. Carl and Lefty served while Grandfather did the best he could without his teeth.

After dinner, Mrs. Robinson read *Tarzan of the Apes* aloud. Suddenly, one of the frogs jumped up onto my hand and did a Tarzan yodel. *He was wearing Grandfather Robinson's teeth.*

"I found them! I found them!" I cried.

Everybody shouted, "Hooray!" except for Wilbur, who did a Tarzan yodel too.

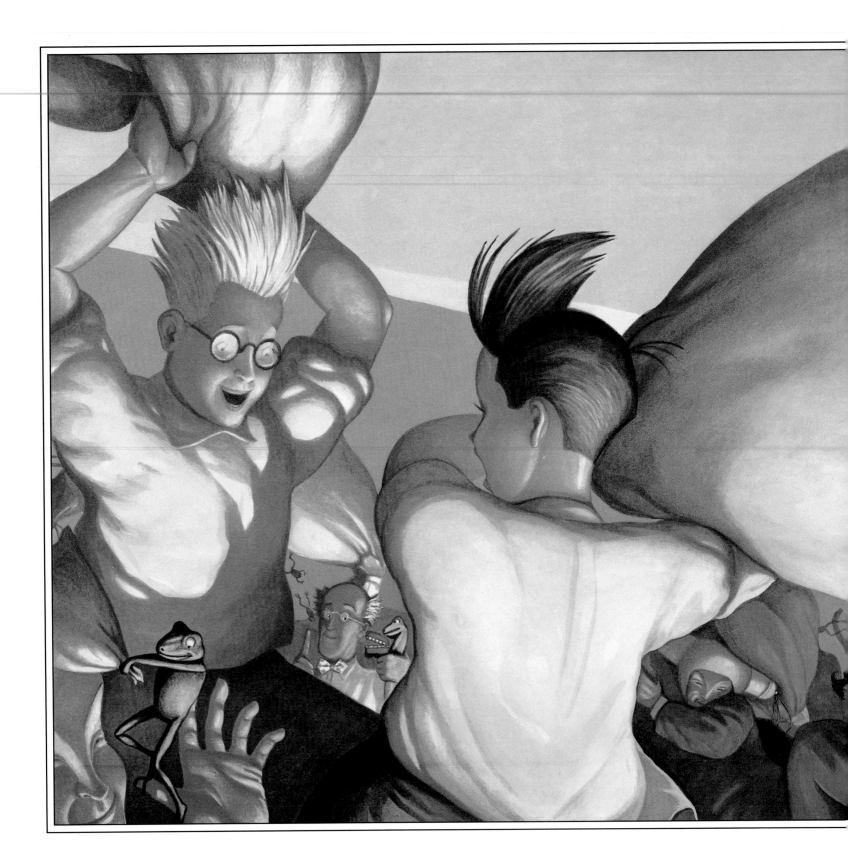

The occasion called for a pillow fight.

Exhausted from the battle, we floated across the lawn and into a tree with the help of Cousin Laszlo's antigravity device. Wilbur and I stayed up while Uncle Art told hair-raising stories about his adventures in outer space, as the frogs played softly on their violins.

The next morning the whole family was out front waving good-bye and singing "Yes, We Have No Bananas," just like they always do.

I was kind of sad to leave, but I was ready to go home for a while.

"Good-bye, Wilbur," I said.

"Sorry it was such a dull day," Wilbur apologized.

"Hey, I had fun," I said.

Wilbur smiled.

The sun was shining brightly as I walked slowly away. I looked back over my shoulder, and there was Wilbur, shooting himself out of Uncle Gaston's cannon with a farewell message: